The Egg Salad Sandwich Incident

By Joe Rhatigan
Illustrated by Emilie Pepin

Publishing Credits

Rachelle Cracchiolo, M.S.Ed., *Publisher*
Conni Medina, M.A.Ed., *Editor in Chief*
Nika Fabienke, Ed.D., *Content Director*
Véronique Bos, *Creative Director*
Shaun N. Bernadou, *Art Director*
Seth Rogers, *Editor*
Valerie Morales, *Associate Editor*
Kevin Pham, *Graphic Designer*

Image Credits

Illustrated by Emilie Pepin

Library of Congress Cataloging-in-Publication Data

Names: Rhatigan, Joe, author. | Pépin, Émilie, illustrator.
Title: The egg salad sandwich incident / by Joe Rhatigan ; illustrated by
 Emilie Pepin.
Description: Huntington Beach, CA : Teacher Created Materials, [2019] |
 Audience: Ages 13 | Audience: Grades 4-6 | Summary: Middle-schooler
 Jesse, pleased when the popular students at his new school invite him to
 their lunch table, must reconsider when their pranks hurt his friend,
 Timothy. Includes "Book Club Questions."
Identifiers: LCCN 2019026457 (print) | LCCN 2019026458 (ebook) | ISBN
 9781644913536 (paperback) | ISBN 9781644914434 (ebook)
Subjects: CYAC: Conduct of life--Fiction. | Popularity--Fiction. |
 Schools--Fiction. | Friendship--Fiction.
Classification: LCC PZ7.R337824 Egg 2019 (print) | LCC PZ7.R337824
 (ebook) | DDC [Fic]--dc23
LC record available at https://lccn.loc.gov/2019026457
LC ebook record available at https://lccn.loc.gov/2019026458

5301 Oceanus Drive
Huntington Beach, CA 92649-1030
www.tcmpub.com

ISBN 978-1-6449-1353-6

Table of Contents

CHAPTER ONE

Kooser the Loser

Jesse's family moved around a lot, so he was used to figuring out new schools. However, he was a little confused that Janet B. Malone Elementary let the fifth and sixth graders sit wherever they wanted at lunchtime instead of with their classes. Eating lunch with your class kept kids, especially new kids, from having to eat lunch alone. So, for the first day in his new school, Jesse ate alone.

It felt like an experiment concocted by the school's science teachers: "Let's study what happens when we let kids choose their own seats at lunch! It will be fascinating."

About midway through his first lonely lunch, a boy sat across from Jesse. The boy took a hand wipe out of his backpack and wiped down the table in front of him before putting down his lunch box. Without even introducing himself, the boy said, "I'm sensitive to germs, OK?"

"Yeah, no problem," Jesse said.

"OK. The cool table is over by the windows. You want to be out of throwing range of them. Otherwise, you may end up in the middle of a potato-puff storm."

Jesse introduced himself, and the boy said, "I'm Timothy Kooser, otherwise known as Kooser the Loser. You'll probably get invited to sit at the cool table one day. If you do, just remember—I was the first kid to say hi to you."

"I won't get invited," Jesse insisted.

"If someone asked me, I'd go in a heartbeat," Timothy replied. "It must be fun to be popular."

Jesse knew there were cliques at every school, and he always tried to avoid them. He found that it was easier to keep your hand down in the classroom and your head down everywhere else. *Don't stand out* was his motto.

He spent the next few days sitting with Timothy at lunch. Jesse got used to him wiping every surface with disinfectant. Timothy also cleaned his hands a lot and talked incessantly about diseases. After a few minutes, Jesse would stop listening and sneak glances over at the cool table. Those kids spent a lot of time making strange mixtures with their milks and juices and iceberg lettuce salads and daring each other to drink them.

CHAPTER TWO

Life at the Cool Table

About a week and a half later, Jesse got too close to the cool table, and before he knew it, someone yelled, "Tater storm!" Potato puffs rained down on him, but instead of running, Jesse used his empty lunch tray as a bat and whacked the tots back at the cool table.

After lunch, in social studies, a boy sitting next to Jesse said, "My name is Tobias, and that was awesome what you did with the potato puffs."

"Thanks, I guess," Jesse said.

"You should sit with us tomorrow."

Jesse said, "Sure. Why not?"

The next day, Tobias introduced Jesse to the cool table kids.

Tobias named a bunch of kids, each with a rhyming nickname, including: Lucy Goosy (because she's silly), Red Ted (because he has red hair), Too-Tall Paul, and Maria Diarrhea.

Jesse took a seat at the end of the table next to No-Nickname Laurie. He asked her, "Where's your rhyming nickname?"

"I guess Tobias can't think of one."

"What about 'Laurie Lavatory' or 'Gory Laurie'?" Jesse suggested.

"Keep *those* names to yourself…if you know what's good for you," Laurie teased.

Jesse laughed but then looked over at where Timothy sat by himself. He wanted to invite Timothy over but knew the kids at the table wouldn't like it. He felt sad and guilty, but he turned away while he decided whether he would drink the concoction his new friends were passing to him.

Tobias said, "It's a mac and cheese chocolate milkshake with grape juice, raisins, graham crackers, and, of course,

potato puffs. The first gulp goes to our newest member...Messy Jesse."

"Drink, drink, drink!" everyone chanted while banging on the table.

Jesse took a small sip, but Tobias said, "Chug it!"

So, he did. It was one of most awful things that had ever passed through his lips, but he knew he had to be cool. The kids got silent as he put the concoction down; they were all waiting for him to say something.

"You must give me the recipe—it's delicious," Jesse said.

The whole table whooped and hollered, welcoming Jesse to the school and the cool table. Jesse couldn't remember the last time he felt this *wanted* by anyone at school, and at that moment, it was easy to forget about Timothy.

CHAPTER THREE

Prank Time

Most times, the cool table kids talked about video games, annoying siblings, and getting in trouble. Sometimes, their antics got too rowdy. But the teachers on lunch duty always seemed to go easy on them. It felt like a private club, and Jesse couldn't believe he was included.

One of Jesse's favorite people at the cool table was Lucy Goosy. Lucy was fearless. She was great at making faces and imitating teachers. She cracked everyone up with her impression of Mr. Freeman, the social studies teacher. She even made fun of Tobias once in a while. The others at the table would never do that. He was their leader.

About a month after Jesse started sitting at the cool table, Tobias had an idea for a prank. He handed out stickers and whispered, "When you get back to class, put a sticker under every mouse. No one will be able to use the computers."

Jesse thought about saying "No, thanks," but he put a few stickers in his pocket. The stickers made him feel included but also something else… something that didn't feel like *himself.*

Everyone at the table seemed really excited about the prank at lunch, but only a couple of kids went through with it. Tobias got away with it by swearing

he didn't do it. Paul managed to sticker half the mouses in the computer lab before getting caught.

After lunch, Jesse and Lucy had math together. When they got there, Mr. Fitz, the math teacher, wasn't in the room yet. It would be easy to put a sticker under the mouse on his desk. Jesse wanted more than anything to prove to his friends that not only was he brave but that he was quick enough to get away with it. Jesse gathered all of his courage, walked to the front of the classroom, and placed a sticker on the bottom of Mr. Fitz's mouse. When Mr. Fitz came in, Jesse was safely back in his seat.

Mr. Fitz never used his computer during class. Jesse had pulled the prank and got away with it! Jesse was a hero, but he didn't feel like one. He worried so much about getting caught that he couldn't eat for two whole days.

The next day at lunch, Tobias called Jesse fearless. Kids patted him on the back and high-fived him in the hallway.

It felt good. But hearing about how Mr. Fitz had to use rubbing alcohol to remove the sticker from his computer mouse made him feel horrible. In fact, he never quite knew how to feel these days.

The sticker incident started a trend. Suddenly, everyone had ideas for pranks. No-Nickname Laurie put glitter on top of the science teacher's door so that when she swung the door open, glitter fell all over her. Tobias hid hard-boiled eggs in several lockers. That one took patience because the eggs didn't start smelling bad until three days later. The more pranks kids pulled, the stricter the teachers got.

The pranks reminded Jesse of his last school. Jesse had told his friend Miguel how much he hated spiders. A few days later, Miguel snuck a plastic spider in his biology textbook. Jesse jumped out of his chair, yelling, when he saw the toy. He remembered how ashamed he felt when he heard everyone—including his teacher—laughing.

CHAPTER FOUR

Potato-Puff Germs

The pranks were getting out of control, but Jesse preferred being one of the kids doing the pranking rather than getting pranked.

A week after the sticker incident, Tobias had an idea for pranking Timothy.

"He hates germs, right? Let's take turns sitting across from him with our potato puffs, and then we lick one and put it on his plate. It will gross him out!"

"That's a bad idea," said Jesse. "He's really anxious about that stuff; and why pick on him, anyway? He didn't do anything to us."

"But he's weird, and it's funny."

Everyone else sided with Tobias. Jesse wanted nothing to do with the prank, so he left the cafeteria, pretending he had to use the bathroom. All he could think about was how he felt when he was pranked.

When he returned, he could see Timothy talking to a teacher. He had tears in his eyes and was gesturing wildly. The kids at the cool table stifled their laughter while pretending to eat their lunches.

Jesse passed by close to Timothy and the teacher, and he heard Timothy explaining what happened.

Later, in science, Jesse tried to explain to Timothy that he wasn't part of the prank.

"Look, I wasn't even there," he whispered.

"But you knew it was going to happen," Timothy hissed. "But don't worry, I didn't include your name when I told on your friends, if that's what you're concerned about."

"I feel terrible about what they did, but they wouldn't listen to me. And as your friend, I have to admit, you bring it on yourself with that germ stuff."

"Yeah, *friend*," Timothy said sarcastically. "Thanks for all of your generous advice."

The next few days at lunch were quiet as Tobias and several other kids served lunch detention. Jesse didn't think it was a big deal, but Tobias was angry and wanted revenge.

"Let it go," Jesse said. "Pranking people isn't fun anymore, anyway."

"No way, mister 'I-gotta-go-to-the-bathroom!' We're going to get revenge on Kooser the Loser. I have a brilliant plan, and you're going to help me with it."

"Count me out," Jesse said.

"Then sit somewhere else."

Jesse didn't move and didn't say anything else as Tobias announced his plan to the table.

CHAPTER FIVE

Germ Warfare

Jesse wasn't sure what to do because he didn't like what Tobias was planning, but he also wasn't keen on sitting somewhere else. These kids were his friends, and he didn't want to lose them over a harmless prank. So, he made up his mind to go along with it.

The next day, everyone at the cool table watched as Timothy wiped his table clean, opened up his lunch bag (he never bought lunch because of the germs), and took out his sandwich. Tobias called the school office from his cell phone and passed it to Laurie, who everyone agreed had the most adult-sounding voice.

"Hello, this is Timothy Kooser's mother," Laurie said into the phone. "Can you please put Timothy on the phone for me?"

A moment later, a voice boomed over the loudspeaker: "Timothy Kooser to the office, please."

Timothy left his sandwich on the table as he walked out of the cafeteria.

Tobias hung up the phone and looked at Jesse. "Go get his sandwich."

"Get it yourself," said Jesse.

"Don't be a nerd-face and get it!" Tobias demanded.

Jesse ran over to Timothy's table, grabbed the sandwich, and brought it back. It was an egg salad sandwich with lettuce and tomatoes.

Tobias said, "Pass it around the table. Each kid has to touch the floor with their finger and then touch their finger to the sandwich. Move fast!"

The sandwich went from kid to kid, and each one lifted the top piece of bread and placed a dirty finger in the egg salad. Jesse hesitated when it was his turn, but he did it. Like before,

none of this felt right, but he didn't think he had any other options.

Paul ran the sandwich back just as Timothy was arriving from the office.

The plan was that after his first bite, Tobias would go over and tell Timothy what was in his sandwich. "It's perfect because no one will believe him," Tobias had said. "You can't prove there are *germs* in his sandwich!"

The whole table was tense with anticipation as Timothy sat down. He picked up his sandwich, which now looked a little mushed up and just as he prepared to take a bite…

Jesse stood up and yelled, "Don't eat that, Timothy! We all touched it."

"What!?" Timothy yelled as he threw the sandwich on the table. Meanwhile, the cool table kids groaned and started yelling at Jesse for ruining the prank.

"Go sit with your new, germy best friend, nerd-face," said Tobias.

Just then, Red Ted walked over to Timothy's table and said, "Nobody touched anything, Timothy. Jesse's just being weird, so ignore him."

"Really?" Timothy asked as he reached for his sandwich again.

Jesse stormed over to Timothy's table and grabbed the egg salad sandwich. "I'm not lying," Jesse said. "Everyone put a dirty finger in it—even me—and now I need to throw it away."

Jesse walked over to the garbage can and threw the sandwich away, knowing he had just lost all of his friends.

He decided to leave the cafeteria so he could find someplace to think, but before he could, someone tapped on his shoulder. It was Mr. Fitz, that day's lunch monitor.

"Jesse, I want you to take a seat with the others at your table. I have a few questions for all of you."

CHAPTER SIX

Grime and Punishment

Jesse sat down next to Tobias, who whispered, "Now, we're all in trouble, nerd-face! This is all your fault."

"OK, children," Mr. Fitz began. "From what I can tell, Timothy's sandwich has been tampered with. I want whoever is responsible to stand up."

Jesse knew he had to accept the consequences for his actions, so he rose from his seat. Nobody else stood.

"Come with me, Jesse."

Outside the cafeteria, Mr. Fitz said, "I know you're a good kid, so I want to know who put you up to this."

Jesse didn't feel like a good kid. He thought about telling on Tobias and the rest of the table, but there was only one way he could answer the question.

"No one, sir. I participated in this prank without anyone making me do anything. It was stupid, and I'm embarrassed I did it."

Jesse's punishment was two weeks of lunch detention. Eating his lunch in the main office during detention gave him time to think about everything that had gone wrong.

The first day of lunch detention, Timothy walked in the office. Jesse got his attention and said, "I'm sorry. The cool table was a quick way of making friends, but it wasn't the best way."

"I'm not interested in your apologies."

"Timothy," Jesse said, "I have an unreasonable fear of spiders."

"Really?" Timothy, smiled. "Well, when I'm talking to you again, remind me to make fun of you."

Two days later, Lucy walked into the office with her lunch.

"What are you doing here?" Jesse asked.

"I confessed to Mr. Fitz that I touched the sandwich, too. I couldn't let you be the only kid with guts." She made a funny face at him, and he laughed.

"I guess we'll both need a new lunch table," Jesse said.

"Who will sit with us?" Lucy asked.

"I think for a while it may just be you and me. But I'll save a seat for Timothy."

They ate their lunches quietly for a moment, and then Lucy said, "You're a good friend."

Jesse responded, "Not yet, but I'm learning."

About Us

The Author
Joe Rhatigan is an author and book editor who occasionally loves sandwiches but hates egg salad. He has written such books as *Everyone Toots*, *I Love a Book*, and dozens more. He lives in Asheville, North Carolina, with a dog named Rooster and the rest of his family.

The Illustrator
Emilie Pepin is an illustrator living in Quebec, Canada. She loves children's illustration and picture books for their limitless creativity, fantastic worlds, and characters. After completing her studies in 2-D animation, Emilie worked for nearly 10 years in the children's video game field as a 2-D artist and art director.